MW01103240

Indian Nations

THE OJIBWA

by
Cathy McCarthy

General Editors
Herman J. Viola and David Jeffery

A Rivilo Book

A Harcourt Company

Austin • New York
www.steck-vaughn.com

Published by Raintree Steck-Vaughn Company, an imprint of the Steck-Vaughn Company

Developed for Steck-Vaughn Company by Rivilo Books
Editor: David Jeffery
Photo Research: Linda Sykes
Design: Barbara Lisenby and Todd Hirshman
Electronic Preparation: Lyda Guz
Native Elder and language advisor: Helen Wassegijig

Raintree Steck-Vaughn Publishers Staff
Publishing Director: Walter Kossmann
Editor: Kathy DeVico

Photo Credits: Richard Olsenius/National Geographic Image Collection: cover; Victoria and Julius Lisi: illustration, pp. 4, 6; Cathy McCarthy: p. 7 top; Lowell Georgia/Corbis: pp. 7 bottom, 21; James P. Rowan: p. 8; Macduff Everton/Corbis: p. 11; Royal Ontario Museum: p. 12 bottom; Milwaukee Public Museum: pp. 12 top, 32 bottom, 34; Library of Congress: p. 13; Tippecanoe County Historical Association, Lafayette, Indiana, gift of Mrs. Cable G. Ball: p. 14; Bettmann/Corbis: pp. 15, 16; Courtesy of Basil Johnston: p. 17 left; Courtesy HarperCollins: p. 17 right; Corbis: p. 18; Courtesy Lorraine Norrgard and James Fortier from the documentary series "Waasaa Inaabidaa-We Look in All Directions," PBS Eight/WDSE TV, Duluth, MN (www.ojibwe.org): pp. 19, 20, 28, 30, 31, 35, 38 bottom, 38 left, 39 top, 41; Ayer Collection, Minnesota Historical Society: pp. 22 bottom left, 22 bottom right, 22 top, 32 right, 33, 35 top (E 97.1 N/R), 42; James Fortier: pp. 23, 39 bottom, 39 middle; Phil Schermeister/Corbis: p. 24; Newberry Library/Superstock: p. 25; National Anthropological Archives/Smithsonian Institution: p. 26; Werner Forman/Corbis: p. 27 bottom; American Museum of Natural History: p. 27 top; David Arnold/National Geographic Society Image Collection: p. 29; National Museum of American Art, Smithsonian Institution/Art Resource: p. 36

Library of Congress Cataloging-in-Publication Data
McCarthy, Cathy
The Ojibwa / by Cathy McCarthy.
p. cm. — (Indian nations)
Includes bibliographical references and index.
ISBN 0-8172-5460-9
1. Ojibwa Indians — History. 2. Ojibwa Indians — Social life and customs.
I. Title. II. Indian nations (Austin, Tex.)
E99.C6 M319 2001
977.004'973—dc21
00-039026

Printed and bound in the United States
2 3 4 5 6 7 8 9 0 LB 04 03 02 01

Cover photo: An Ojibwa boy dances at a powwow in Canada.

Contents

Pronunciation of some Ojibwa words are found in the Glossary.

Creation Story

The Creator, whom the Ojibwa people call **Gitchi Manitou**, created the world and all that was in it from a vision that he had. He sent the birds to the East, West, North, and South to spread the seeds of life so that all things would grow. Then he created beings to swim in the water, and to crawl and walk the Earth. He told all these beings to live in balance with one another, in a circle that would allow them to thrive. Finally, the Creator gathered fire, water, air, and earth. He blew a living spirit into them through a seashell called a **Megis**. From the union of these four elements, original man was created and placed on the Earth. The word **Anishinaabe**, which is the name the people call themselves, celebrates the gift of life given to these, the original people. Ani means "from," Nishina means "lowered to the Earth," and Abe indicates the male of a species.

After some time, the Earth was filled with people who forgot to live in harmony with the rest of creation. So the Creator caused the waters of the Earth to flood in order to purify it.

A woman named Geezhigo-Quae (Sky Woman) was married to a godlike spirit called a **Manitou**. At the time of the great flood, Sky Woman was pregnant with the Manitou's twin children but was very lonely and homesick for the Earth below. The animals and birds that survived the flood and floated upon the water invited her to come down from the sky and make her home on the back of a turtle.

The muskrat gives Sky Woman, who is soon to have twins, some soil from the bottom of the floodwaters.

She asked the animals to dive beneath the floodwaters and bring her back a piece of soil. Only the muskrat was able to hold his breath long enough to reach the bottom and return with the soil in his paws. Geezhigo-Quae spread the soil around the rim of the turtle's shell. She then breathed life and growth into the soil. The turtle's shell began to expand, and the soil took root to form the continent of North America. This continent is known today among the Ojibwa, as well as other tribes, as Turtle Island.

The Seven Fires Prophecy

A long time ago, the Creator sent seven prophets to a peaceful tribe of people called the Ojibwa. They lived in villages along the north Atlantic Ocean coast. The seven prophets brought their **prophecies** in the form of **Seven Fires**. These fires did not burn hot like campfires, but were more like flames in the sky bearing messages for the people.

The First Fire prophet told the Ojibwa to rise up and leave their home. He told them to follow the sacred Megis (seashell) to a land chosen for them by the Creator. At the beginning of their journey and at the end, they would find an island shaped like a turtle. The Ojibwa would know they had reached their destination when they came to a place where food grew on water. If they did not do what the prophet said, they would be destroyed.

The second prophet told them in the time of the Second Fire that the Ojibwa would camp by a large body of water, and they would wish to go no farther. A child would remind them that they had not yet reached their destination.

The prophet of the First Fire told the Ojibwa people to follow the sacred Megis seashell (right) to a place where food grew on water. Wild rice grows on the edge of Leech Lake, Minnesota (below), and Ojibwa harvest it.

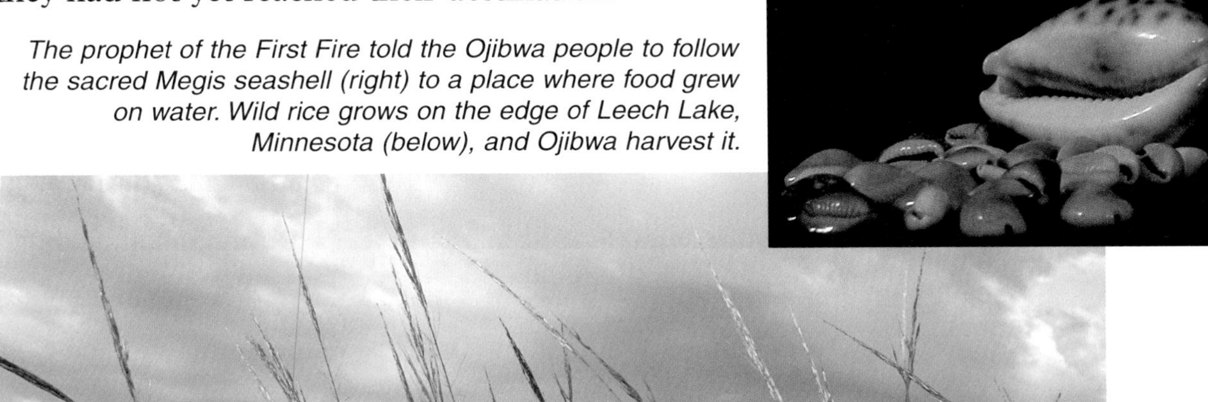

The third prophet said that in the time of his fire, the people would start their journey again and finally come to the place where food grew on water.

The fourth prophet came in the form of two men. They told of the coming of a light-skinned race. They said that if the light-skinned ones came with wonderful gifts, there would come a time of change that would be good for the people. But if the light-skinned visitors came bearing the face of death, or carrying weapons with them, they would destroy the people and the land.

The sixth prophet told Ojibwa elders to hide the sacred scrolls and bundles in cliffs by a great inland sea. Lake Superior (left) is the largest lake in North America.

The fifth prophet talked about a time of great struggle when light-skinned ones would come into their villages and promise to save them from all troubles and give them great joy. The prophet warned that this promise would be false.

The Sixth Fire would be a time of great loss. Children would turn against their elders. They would forget the traditional ways and forget their language. Sickness and death would descend upon them. Fearing the loss of their souls, the elders would take all the sacred birch bark scrolls, all the **sacred bundles** and relics, and place them in a hollowed-out log. The elders would hide the log in the side of a cliff by a great inland sea. These

sacred things would lie in wait for a time when the people could practice their traditional ways without fear or punishment.

The seventh prophet said that the young people would search for the log that was buried in the cliff. They would seek out the elders to help them. The young people's task would be hard, but if they stuck to it, a sacred fire would be lit to guide the people.

In the end, the Ojibwa people would offer the light-skinned ones, who were now their neighbors, the choice of two paths; one leading to the spirit, the other continuing the destruction of the Earth. If they chose the first path, the fire of peace and brotherhood would be lit. If they chose the second, then suffering and death would come to all people of the Earth.

Key Historical Events

Just as the First Fire promised, sometime between A.D. 900 and 1400, the Ojibwa left their home on the Atlantic Coast. They moved inland, along the St. Lawrence River to settle along the northern and southern shores of Lake Michigan and Lake Superior.

As in the story of the Second Fire, the people first settled on an island shaped like a turtle, called Mackinac. Their final destination, foretold in the Third Fire, was Madeline Island, or Mooningwanekaning in Ojibwa, near the western tip of Lake Superior. It was here that the Ojibwa people found wild rice growing up through the water along the marshy shores. Ojibwa people living in this region are known today as the Chippewa.

Smaller groups of people broke away from the main group and set up communities all along the St. Lawrence River and the Great Lakes. These people, who would be known later as the Abenaki, the Ottawa, and the Potowatomi, formed an alliance with the Ojibwa. They did so to protect the people from other tribes and to ensure that the prophecies of the Seven Fires were followed.

When French explorers started making their way inland during the early 1600s, they began trading metal goods, beads, cloth, and firearms for beaver and other animal pelts. At first the Ojibwa traded through the Ottawa. But as the explorers made their way farther into the interior, the Ojibwa began trading directly with them.

The Ojibwa believed that these light-skinned men were the first group foretold in the Fourth Fire, because they brought goods that made their lives easier. In turn, the Ojibwa taught the

Ron Paquin makes a birch bark canoe. He is a Chippewa, another name for the Ojibwa.

French how to build canoes and how to hunt and survive in the wilderness. They also allowed the explorers to marry into their clans.

Diseases such as **smallpox**, **tuberculosis**, **bubonic plague**, and **cholera** were unknown in North America until the French arrived. The Ojibwa began to get sick. Their immune systems were not prepared to handle these diseases, and they could not be cured by the herbs and plants they had always used against sickness. More than half the Ojibwa population died within the first fifty years of contact with Europeans. The Ojibwa believed that these diseases were brought by the second group foretold in the Fourth Fire.

About the same time that diseases struck the villages, Catholic priests, whom the Ojibwa called **Blackrobes**, arrived. The priests told the people that their traditional beliefs were wrong and that they were falling sick because they would not believe in the Christian God. The people noticed that some of those who left the village to live among the light-skinned ones survived the diseases and never got sick again. Surely it was because they had given up their ways and become Christian, the people thought. And so to save themselves from death, many people converted to Christianity.

Father Jacques Marquette, in the first canoe, and explorer Louis Jolliet, in the second, were the first Europeans to travel a long stretch of the middle Mississippi River. They were probably guided by Ojibwa scouts, as shown in this painting.

The Ojibwa holy people, called **Mide** (MEE-day), warned that the message brought by the Blackrobes was the false message spoken of in the Fifth Fire. But the outbreaks of disease and the attraction to European trade goods turned many people away from their traditional life. Guns were especially popular. With them they could hunt better. And with guns, the Ojibwa could fight their traditional enemies, the Lakota Sioux, the Sauk and Fox, and the Iroquois.

The European demand for furs, especially beaver, plus the loss of traditional values led to overhunting. Soon animals hunted for both food and trade grew scarce. Encouraged by the

In a scene woven into birch bark, an Ojibwa warrior with a gun, on the left, and one with a war club, on the right, have defeated one of their enemies—a Mohawk of the Iroquois Confederation holding a bow and arrow.

This scene of a fight on Lake Superior between Ojibwa and Fox warriors shows that Indian nations also had conflicts with each other and not just with Europeans.

demand of European fur traders, tribes fought each other for the few remaining animals.

As food grew scarce, the Ojibwa depended more and more on Europeans to give them tools to hunt better and to share what they now grew on farms. The Europeans used the situation to take more land and drive the remaining Ojibwa onto **reservations**. Weakened by disease and war, and forgetting their traditions and skills, the people had little choice but to do as the Europeans said.

By 1759 Britain won control of North America, and the French lost most of their influence. More than the French, the British viewed Indians as dangerous savages and their cultures as unworthy of respect. To expand their own settlements, the British began to drive the Ojibwa and other Indians off their ancestral lands and set about controlling them by force or with the threat of starvation.

Although they were fierce and successful warriors, the Ojibwa saw that they were no match for the numbers and

The Potowatomi, who, with the Ottawa, had once been joined to the Ojibwa, gathered to hear a sermon before they were forced to move west by an unfair treaty in 1837.

weapons of the light-skinned ones. So many times, the Ojibwa decided that rather than fight, they would enter into treaties and trade with Europeans and, later, Americans and Canadians. For the most part, the Ojibwa did not choose sides in the American Revolution, nor did they choose sides in the War of 1812. They fought on both sides.

A series of treaties, beginning in 1785, gradually pushed the Ojibwa westward into the Great Lakes region in what are now Minnesota and Wisconsin. Eventually though, American settlers forced those Ojibwa to make treaties and give up much of their land. In the same way, the movement of settlers westward in Canada led to treaties that took land from the Ojibwa along the northern shores of the Great Lakes.

The governments of the United States and Canada decided that the best way to deal with all Indians was to force them to adopt European ways. Laws were made that forbade the practice of Indian traditional ways, the speaking of Indian language, and the wearing of Indian clothes and hairstyles. Sacred bundles containing the bones and relics of ancestors were destroyed. Pipes, scrolls, and drums used in Indian ritual were stolen and sent to museums.

By the middle of the 19th century, the Canadian and United States governments began to remove Indian children from their homes and families and sent them to live and study at boarding schools run by the state or by religious orders, such as the

Jesuits. If the children spoke their own language, refused to worship the Christian god, or disobeyed the teachers in any way, they were severely punished.

Some young people emerged from that school system mentally and physically damaged and drifted to the cities, where they poisoned themselves with alcohol and drugs. Although the boarding schools were closed by the 1970s, many Native Americans still suffer the lingering effects of isolation from family and community they felt during their childhood and teenage years. The Ojibwa saw these events as the coming of the Sixth Fire.

In the 1960s a spirit of change blew across North America. The civil rights and antiwar movements made young people bold in expressing their opinions. A new generation of young Ojibwa leaders such as Dennis Banks, Clyde and Vernon Bellecourt, Harold Goodsky, and George Mitchell helped form the **American Indian Movement (AIM)**. They demanded

Vernon Bellecourt, a leader of the American Indian Movement (AIM) spoke to students at Kent State University in 1973. The ceremonies honored Kent State students who had been killed in May 1970, protesting the Vietnam War, by gunfire from the Ohio National Guard.

In 1973, Indians stood guard near a Catholic church in Wounded Knee, South Dakota. Members of AIM took control of the town to remember the slaughter of Indians there in 1890 and to protest poor treatment of Indian people today.

that the United States government live up to the terms of the many treaties it had made and then broken. They challenged old leaders in reservation governments who were known for stealing money and terrorizing their own people. The AIM organization promoted and funded legal action, national protest demonstrations, and information campaigns against both state and federal governments. Members of AIM stopped the digging up and the theft of Indian remains in sacred burial grounds.

The actions of the young Indian leaders resulted in many positive consequences. Some ancestral land, never signed away in treaties, was returned. Skeletal remains of ancestors were returned from the vaults of museums. More importantly, there was a return of Indian dignity and pride. The actions of some AIM leaders also led to violent confrontation with the government. The most important of these confrontations was in 1973 at Wounded Knee, South Dakota. A group of Indian activists occupied the Wounded Knee site, where in 1890 about 300 Dakota Sioux had been gunned down by U.S. troops. The activists of 1973 wanted to draw attention to what they thought was shameful treatment of Indian people both in the past and in the present. The confrontation turned violent. After 1973's 71-day occupation was over, two people had been killed; 12 had been wounded, including two U.S. Marshals; and nearly 1,200 people had been arrested.

Since the Wounded Knee incident, Ojibwa leaders have chosen more peaceful means to pursue their claims with the American and Canadian governments. They have organized health care and healing circles to help those who suffered in **residential schools**. The leaders have developed businesses to employ their people, and they have moved toward self-government in the hopes of having an Indian nation within a nation.

The Ojibwa leaders have sought the help of their elders and are reviving the traditional ways of their sacred (**Midewiwin**) society. Those rebuilding their tribal identity and their pride are working hard for the fulfillment of the Seventh Fire.

Finally, the Ojibwa people have invited all the members of the nation to seek his or her own spirit through the understanding of traditional ways and history. Norval Morrisseau, an artist, Edward Benton-Benai, a traditional teacher, and Basil Johnston, an author and storyteller, are among those who now teach and interpret Ojibwa spiritual traditions to all who are interested.

Of Ojibwa and German-American heritage, Louise Erdrich (above) is known as one of America's finest writers. Ojibwa scholar, author, and storyteller, Basil Johnston (right), helps keep alive Ojibwa language, history, culture, and customs.

Way of Life

Dwellings and Home Life

The Ojibwa built several different types of homes, depending on the time of year and what materials were easily available to them for construction. But, overall, the people preferred building and living in a **wigwaum** (wigwam).

The wigwaum was a round-topped lodge that was oblong in shape. It was usually between 9 and 12 feet (2.7 and 3.7 m) long, 10 feet (3m) wide, and 5 to 6 feet (1.5 to 1.8 m) high. There was one entrance that always faced the east, because this

Ojibwa build a wigwaum in a drawing made in 1884. Saplings were bent into a light but sturdy framework. The framework was covered with mats made from bulrushes. The roof was made of birch bark strips sewn together.

A modern wigwaum is built in the traditional way. Although they could still be used, today's wigwaums are made more to keep Ojibwa cultural history alive than as places to live in.

is where the sun rose and where the people believed that all life began. The wigwaum was built on ground that sloped downward in the corner opposite the entrance. Thin drainage ditches were dug along the back of the lodge in the same direction as the slope. This helped water drain out during wet weather.

The frame of the wigwaum was formed with easily bent saplings (young trees) of the ironwood tree. These were covered with mats woven from the leaves and stalks of bulrushes. Wide strips of birch bark were sewn together and used as a roof. In winter, a layer of bulrush matting was placed on the inside of the wigwaum to keep out the cold. An open space was left in the middle of the roof to allow smoke from the cooking fire to escape. At first, the people hung animal skins across the opening as a door. After the Europeans came, the Ojibwa preferred to hang woolen blankets. A heavy stick was sewn across the bottom of the skin or blanket to hold it down.

Inside the wigwaum, the people slept and sat on mats made of the leaves of bulrushes and placed around the fire pit. They either rolled up their personal belongings or kept them in woven cedar baskets stored along the walls.

Several families, made up of two and three generations, lived together in one wigwaum. Bedding consisted of blankets and animal hides tanned with the hair left on them. Sometimes the people made mattresses and pillows of cloth filled with duck feathers. Only food to be cooked that day was kept just inside the entrance on a wood frame. The rest would be kept outside on another frame. Supplies of wood, wild rice, corn, dried meat, and extra clothing were stored in pits lined with birch bark or in small lean-tos, or open sheds, close by.

During the summer, people stayed outside most of the time. When they were away hunting or fishing, or if it was time to make maple sugar or harvest the wild rice beds, families would either build a lighter version of the wigwaum or construct lean-tos at their temporary camps. In the winter, when the days were short and the weather bitterly cold, they would gather around the fire to keep warm. They would live off the food they had collected during the summer months and what meat they could get by hunting and fishing.

In winter, wigwaums were sometimes covered with hides. Snow helped the home stay warm, while blankets and hides were good, warm covers to snuggle under.

Clothing and Personal Gear: Women's Clothing

For working in the bush gathering food or firewood, women wore a dress and leggings made of deerskin. Two skins were sewn at the shoulders with thread made from fibers of a plant called **nettle-stalk** or from **deer sinew**, or tendons. The dress was then pulled over the head and shoulders and tied at the waist with a belt. Leggings that went from just below the knee to the ankle were made by sewing the skin into the shape of a tube.

Dressed in buckskin, a woman works on a cradleboard. Women used them to carry their babies.

When traders brought wool and cotton broadcloth to the frontier, women's wear took on a new style. Five dollars' worth of pelts bought a length of fabric from armpit to ankle with an extra yard thrown in. The traders also supplied tiny glass beads, braided coils of colored thread, and wool for decorating the broadcloth.

A broadcloth dress was made by sewing the cloth into a tube shape. An extra yard was sewn lengthwise up the front so that a panel extended up like an overall bib. Straps were sewn around the shoulders to hold the dress up. The front panel was decorated with floral designs embroidered in both beads and colored thread. Colored braided coils of wool and thread were sewn around the bottom as a border. A separate piece of broadcloth, roughly 18 to 20 inches (46 to 50 cm) wide, was sewn together at the lengthwise ends to form cuffs around the lower arms. It was then worn across the back like a shawl. Around their heads, women would tie a band of fur decorated with bone, shell, or beads. As shawls and kerchiefs became available, women wore them more than headbands.

Both men and women wore their hair long, because they believed that life forces flowed through the hair shafts, giving them strength and courage. For everyday life, women preferred holding their hair back in a single ponytail. On special occasions, they would make two braids near their ears and cover them almost completely with otter skins.

The traditional Ojibwa **moccasin** for both men and women was made of a single piece of deer or moose hide with a puckered seam up the front and a plain seam up the back. In fact the Europeans derived the name "Ojibwa" and its other version, "Chippewa," from the Ojibwa word for puckered.

These Ojibwa moccasins are decorated for wearing on special occasions.

By the late 1800s, women dressed as American women did. They wore traditional clothing for ceremonial occasions only.

Men's Clothing

Before European contact, men wore deerhide leggings that extended from the upper thigh to the ankle. They wore a **breechcloth** over the leggings. The leggings were held in place with a belt drawn through loops attached to the upper edge of the leggings. The breechcloth was also held in place by the same belt. Woven sashes ornamented with porcupine quills and later with beads and long colored

Buckskin leggings (left) were tough, practical, and handsome. Breechcloths (right) worn by men in the summer were also practical. But this one is finely decorated and probably would not have been worn every day.

At modern powwows Indian people share traditions and borrow styles of dress from each other. For many, eagle feathers are sacred, as well as symbols of great deeds.

sinew or woolen tassels were tied just below the knee over the leggings. Shirts were originally made from deerskin, sewn in the same way as a woman's dress. In the summer, only a breechcloth was worn. Broadcloth eventually took the place of deerskin for making leggings and breechcloths. The edge of the breechcloth was often decorated with ribbon and beadwork.

Men also wore headbands of fur and later of woven beads. Eagle feathers were tucked into the bands to show rank and service to the community. On ceremonial occasions, and especially if dancing was involved, men liked to wear a crown woven of stiff moose hair.

Men took particular pride in their hair. Women would comb and rub it with bear grease or deer tallow, or fat, to keep it smooth and shiny. The men preferred wearing it in two braids and often cut the front into a fringe over their foreheads. Older men often wore a short braid at each temple with the rest in two braids.

Brass armbands and bracelets were popular items exchanged for furs. Men would wear many of them at once. Young men sometimes liked to wear narrow bands of fur around their necks and ankles, the ends hanging and decorated with beads.

Woolen blankets became popular wear for both men and women after Europeans arrived. In fact, blankets were so popular that Ojibwa accepted them in exchange for land. Sometimes blankets were made into winter coats with pointed hoods. But in all types of weather, men wore blankets ceremonially over

one shoulder and under the other arm, with the remaining length drawn closely around the waist. Women wrapped the blanket around them like a tight skirt and fastened it with a belt. The upper part of the blanket was then thrown loosely around the arms or used for carrying a baby on the back between the shoulders.

Food

The Ojibwa believe that **Nanaboozhoo**, an important Manitou, appeared to them in the form of different animals. The animals taught them to identify plants in their environment for food and medicine. At the end of the Third Fire, when they came to the place where food grew in water, the Creator showed them how to collect and prepare wild rice. To thank the

To harvest wild rice, you need a canoe and at least one stick. When you knock the rice stalks with a stick, ripe grains fall into the boat.

Creator, the Ojibwa called the rice **manomin**, which translates to "holy seed." It grew from lake bottoms to arch above the water along some shores of Lake Superior and other smaller lakes and marshy areas. In September, the rice was harvested by people in canoes. They paddled among the plants and beat the overhanging stalks so that the rice fell into the bottom of the boat. When the rice grains were brought onshore, young men and women gently danced on the rice to break the outer shells to separate them from the edible grains inside.

Wild rice was a main staple of the Ojibwa, and it is still harvested in much the same way as it has always been. Many people, Indians and non-Indians alike, consider wild rice to be one of the best tasting grains to eat.

Besides wild rice, the Ojibwa grew corn in the late summer and gathered maple syrup in the spring. They gathered wild berries of all kinds, wild potatoes, acorns and other nuts, and grew pumpkins. Herbs such as wild mint, wild ginger, raspberry leaves, spruce, and wild cherry were used to make tea as well as to season food.

Animals were considered a gift from the Creator. The Ojibwa ate practically everything they could catch except for marten, a fur-bearing animal similar to but larger than

About 1840, American artist Seth Eastman painted a view of a Chippewa (Ojibwa) sugar camp on the shore of a Great Lake, where sap from sugar maples was boiled into syrup. This is a colored etching of Eastman's painting.

a weasel. The Ojibwa believed that when someone ate a certain animal, he or she would take on its personality and character. Since the Ojibwa considered the marten to be sneaky and vicious, no one would eat it.

Out of respect for the **Sacred Circle** of life, and to ensure a continuous food supply, hunters avoided killing females or young animals. They also avoided taking fish during their spawning season. Every part of the animal was used for food, clothing, medicine, or tools.

In a photograph taken before 1930, a Chippewa (Ojibwa) woman is shown drying fish. This is a good way to preserve the meat without refrigeration.

Spiritual Life

The Ojibwa did not separate spiritual life from the rest of life. For example, a person could not go on a deer hunt until he first prayed to the deer. He prayed that the deer would choose to cross his path and give its life for himself and his family. When the hunter killed the deer, he offered it tobacco to thank it. The hunter's family would not eat meat from the deer until they, too, had thanked the deer for its sacrifice and thanked the Creator for the hunter's skill. They would also thank the deer for being in the Sacred Circle of life. Deer and people and all things were in and part of the Sacred Circle.

In this way, everything the Ojibwa did was a religious act. Each act was a prayer to the Creator and a step within the Sacred Circle. Because of this way of thinking and praying, every act had to be made as perfect as possible and be done with the utmost respect. The Ojibwa called this process "walking in the sacred manner."

Some Ojibwa became shamans, or Mide, often called "medicine men" by Europeans. Only children identified by the Mide as possessing special gifts were allowed to enter the sacred (Midewiwin) Society and practice

Holy men, or shamans, called Mide (above) were chosen as children and carefully trained. As grown men they joined the secret Midewiwin Society. Its seating plan was recorded on a strip of birch bark (right).

healing. Once chosen, the student would be taught by a special guide. Students would become full shamans, or Mide, only after their individual teachers and spirit guides died.

Practicing medicine meant using herbs to cure specific diseases, to relieve chronic conditions, and to stop pain. Disease was considered an outward sign of imbalance and turmoil in the spirit of the sick person. So, in order to cure someone of a disease, the Mide sought to understand the underlying mental and spiritual causes of sickness. They did this by interpreting the dreams of the sick. Curing sickness came when the spirit was healed so the body could heal.

The Ojibwa gathered plants for many purposes: to use for food, to dye clothing, to help heal injuries, and to cure diseases.

Family Life

Children

To the Ojibwa, children were gifts of the Creator. So children were treated with great respect. They were carefully watched over and cared for and were given freedom to explore and play. They were guided and taught with gentleness.

For the first months of their lives, babies were tightly wrapped in blankets or skins and then laced into cradleboards to keep their legs and arms growing straight. Toys and charms were hung from an arc over the head of the cradleboard to keep the baby amused. The cradleboard was taken everywhere by the mother and propped up wherever she stopped to work so that the baby could watch or sleep.

Babies were held in cradleboards, and their mothers took them everywhere. Children learned from seeing the world, and their mothers kept watch over them.

Children stayed close to their mothers and the elders of the family until they were seven years old. They were taught not to whine or cry in case there was ever a need to hide from an enemy. Children were also taught to respect fire and not to wander away from the village. Despite all the care given, many children died in the harsh environment of the northern woodlands from accident and from disease, especially those diseases brought by Europeans.

Teaching and Learning

Passing on knowledge and tradition from one generation to another was very important to the Ojibwa. The purpose of teaching was twofold: to prepare men and women to take care of their everyday needs and to enlighten their spirits or inner beings. The community at large and those who taught encouraged all members to use their own special gifts.

Elders taught about life through stories and myths passed down to them from their elders. Children were left to draw

A father teaches his son how to make arrows at Wa-swa-going ("place where they spear fish with torches") in Wisconsin. This Ojibwa village was re-created as it was before Europeans came for a film produced by PBS, the Public Broadcasting System.

their own meaning from the stories so that they might develop a sense of individuality.

Children between birth and seven years were taught by women and elders and learned the basics for survival. After that, boys went with the men to learn hunting and fishing, while the girls stayed with their mothers and elders to learn household arts and skills, planting and harvesting, and making clothing and tools. Finally, women learned the duties of becoming wives and mothers, while men looked for guidance in sacred visions and direction from their animal spirits.

A girl watches as her mother prepares a meal at Wa-swa-going. In traditional times, Ojibwa girls learned from their mothers how to plant and harvest vegetables, how to make clothing and tools, and how to prepare themselves to be wives and mothers.

Toys

Ojibwa children used whatever they could find to make toys. Berries were strung on nettle fiber twine for necklaces. Norway pine needles were woven together to make tiny snowshoes or thin necklaces. Like natural blackboards, lichens made fine surfaces on which to scrape designs like those found on the various baskets and bags of the adults.

Little girls made tiny versions of wooden tools and fashioned mats and roof coverings for dollhouses from bits of birch bark and firewood. Clay found on the riverbank was good for molding animals and dolls. Bulrush roots could be carved to make toy ducks that floated on water. When a boy turned six or seven, his father would make a little bow and blunt arrow to get him used to the idea of hunting.

Mothers and grandmothers made dolls out of a number of materials for their young daughters. They would start with simple forms cut from bark and then replace these with willow and grass forms as the girl got older. Eventually a girl would receive a doll made of a blanket or a piece of broadcloth, stuffed with moss or animal hair. The girl would learn sewing and beadwork skills by making doll clothes and decorating them.

Girls had fun playing with beaded dolls.

Sports and Games

All Ojibwa children learned to be excellent swimmers at a young age. A game of marbles, consisting of little round stones collected on the beach, was always a popular way to pass the afternoon after a swim.

In the "moccasin game," mostly played by grown-ups, musket balls were hidden in pouches that looked like moccasins. The guesser used a stick to point to the pouch that he hoped held the silver musket ball. Good guess, you win! Bad guess—too bad!

Children loved to play a form of hide-and-seek called me-e-mem-gwe (butterfly). Instead of counting to ten and calling out "Ready-or-not, here I come," the seeker would pinch his nose with his fingers and sing "me-e-mem-gwe, show me where to go."

In the winter, boys would make a single ski from a thin piece of wood bark and surf down steep hills. Another winter game involved throwing a stick called a snow snake across crusted snow to see who could send it the farthest.

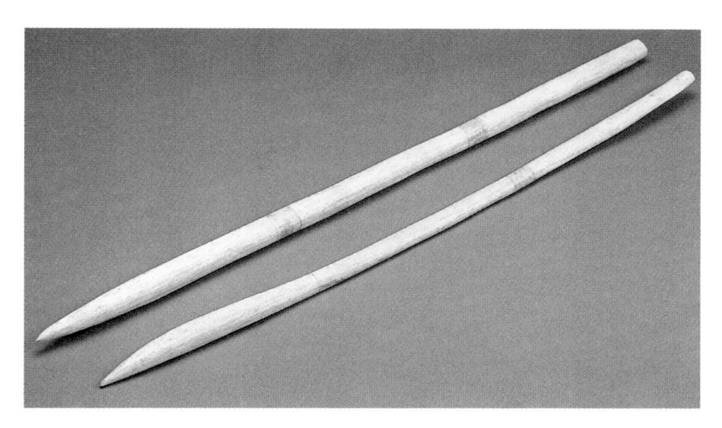

For winter fun, Ojibwa children played "snow snake." They found a really good stick, peeled the bark off, and made the surface smooth. They each slid the snow snake along the top of the crusted snow. The person who slid it the farthest won.

Tribal Society

Political and Social Systems

From the time of the great migration to today, the Ojibwa people have lived in small, scattered communities. This gave rise to a system of government close to the people.

Survival depended on fulfilling five essential needs. These were leadership, defense, sustenance (food), teaching, and medicine. The Ojibwa formed clans called **dodaem** that had the primary responsibility for providing these needs. Each clan chose the spirit of an animal to represent it. Ideally, each community would have at least one representative clan for each need, but this did not always happen.

People were born into the clans like children today are born into families. Instead of inheriting a last name, Ojibwa children took the clan animal name. So to make sure that close relatives did not marry each other, men and women had to marry outside of their own clans.

In 1910, a council leader spoke to a gathering of Chippewas. A leader's role was to represent the community's wishes, not to give orders. If the community did not like the leader, they chose a new one.

Leadership

The Ojibwa chose the crane as the animal symbol of leadership. They recognized in this bird qualities that best defined a great leader. The call of a crane was unique and commanded the attention of all who heard it. Yet it was seldom heard. As such, a leader's role was to exercise command only when it was absolutely needed.

A leader's source of power came from the strength of his character and his ability to persuade and reflect the desires of the community as a whole. If he did not live up to these qualities, the community in council would choose a new leader.

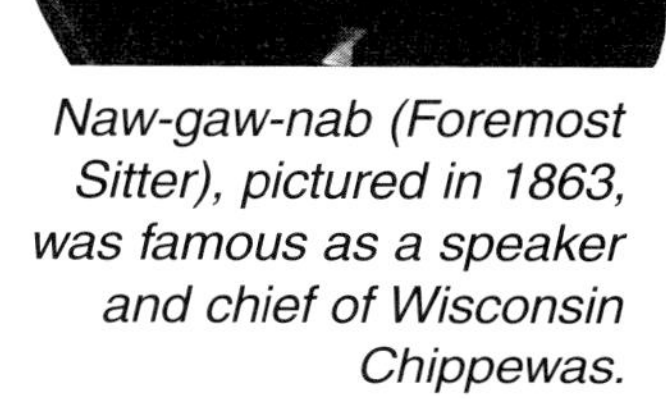

Naw-gaw-nab (Foremost Sitter), pictured in 1863, was famous as a speaker and chief of Wisconsin Chippewas.

The Ojibwa chose an **ogimah**, or chief, to serve and lead them only when help was needed. Individuals were free to join in the group or remain outside of it. Once a crisis was past, there was no longer a need for the organization of people or the skills of a leader, so the group would disband.

Sustenance

The most highly honored job was that of hunter. Hunting called upon the important skills of observation, to track an animal; endurance, to follow the track through dense forest

In some ways hunting in the winter was very hard. It was cold. There were no leaves to hide behind. You could not move fast wearing snowshoes. But there were good points as well. Tracking was easier in snow. Animals could not hide as easily, and many could not run as fast to escape.

and bad weather; patience, to creep up within killing distance; accuracy, to hit the target with bow and arrow; and strength, to carry the kill back to the village.

Every boy went through a period of training to become a hunter. This included learning the character and nature of the animals he would hunt. It also involved building and repairing the tools he would use, and strengthening his body. When a boy made his first kill, the entire village celebrated with a feast and with a special ceremony.

Defense

The Ojibwa regarded warriors as a necessary evil. Conflict and the need to prove oneself in battle were generally the concerns of young men. Warriors were not allowed to be leaders, except in times of danger or crisis.

When warriors took on an enemy, they did not follow a common goal such as winning land or destroying the enemy. To the individual warrior, battle was simply the means of proving courage and gaining standing in the community.

In the 1830s artist George Catlin painted a portrait of Fast Dancer, a Chippewa warrior. He looks very fierce with his face paint and headdress, but he is also wearing peace medals. They were given to Indians as tokens of friendship by American explorers such as Lewis and Clark. The medals bore the face of the President of the United States, like today's nickel shows the face of President Thomas Jefferson.

Contemporary Life

Today more than 190,000 people in North America are officially registered Ojibwa. Twenty-two separate Ojibwa groups are recognized by the United States government, and 130 are recognized by Canada.

Some of these groups live on reservations such as Sandy Lake and White Earth in the United States, and Manitoulin and Ipperwash in Canada. Some of the reservations act as sovereign nations within the country they occupy. This means that they have the right to make and enforce laws, to collect taxes for their own use, and to elect leaders without interference from other governments.

Ojibwa (Chippewa) reservations are found throughout the northern plains states as well as many areas in neighboring Canadian provinces.

Within the reservations, traditional ways are now openly practiced as well as Christian religions and North American lifestyles. Tribal members have developed businesses based on traditional activities, such as growing wild rice and making maple syrup. Organization of information on the Internet, film-making, and developing arts and vacation resorts are some of the new businesses that are springing up.

Sometimes money is awarded as a result of claims that different tribes file with the governments of Canada and the United States. This money is either distributed among tribal members or is used to start businesses where everyone shares in the profits.

Still, there is a lot of unemployment and poverty on reservations. This is because reservations tend to be too far away from cities for members to commute to jobs. And there isn't enough to keep people employed on the reservation itself. Without a way to make money, reservations also lack basic needs such as hospitals, theaters, and shopping malls.

Some traditions, like collecting maple sap for syrup (left) keep on going by themselves. Others need to be revived. Nick Hockings (below, at left), James Fortier, and Lorraine Norrgard work together on the Ojibwa historical film "Waasaa Inaabidaa—We Look in All Directions."

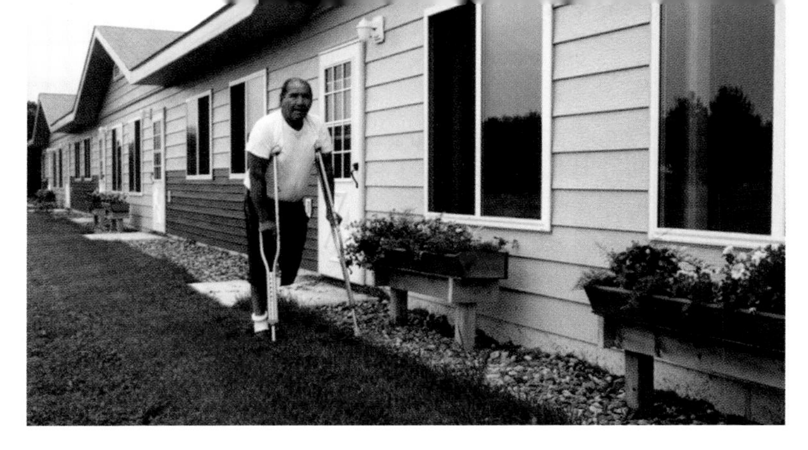

Housing for older Ojibwa people brings warmth, safety, and pride to many who may not have had those benefits before.

To be close to their work, many Ojibwa people have moved into cities far from the reservation. Without the common community and family found on the reservation, these uprooted Indian people may develop feelings of isolation and separation. Such stress, which cannot be shared with others, often leads to social problems such as drinking, drug use, spousal abuse, and early death. All too often, many Indian people end up in prison, while others die young or violently.

To fight against these tragic situations and give hope to the poor and young, some tribes have been able to set up cultural centers and support services for their people in the cities. Tribal people are grouping together in neighborhoods to form their own distinct communities. As these grow, more help can be offered to more people.

Native cultural events, such as powwows, are held every year now in major cities and in many rural areas. Indian community sports teams bring people together as do music and art schools. The Ojibwa, like other Indian communities, are organizing to solve the problem of isolation, to restore a sense of balance, and to bring friends and family into the Sacred Circle.

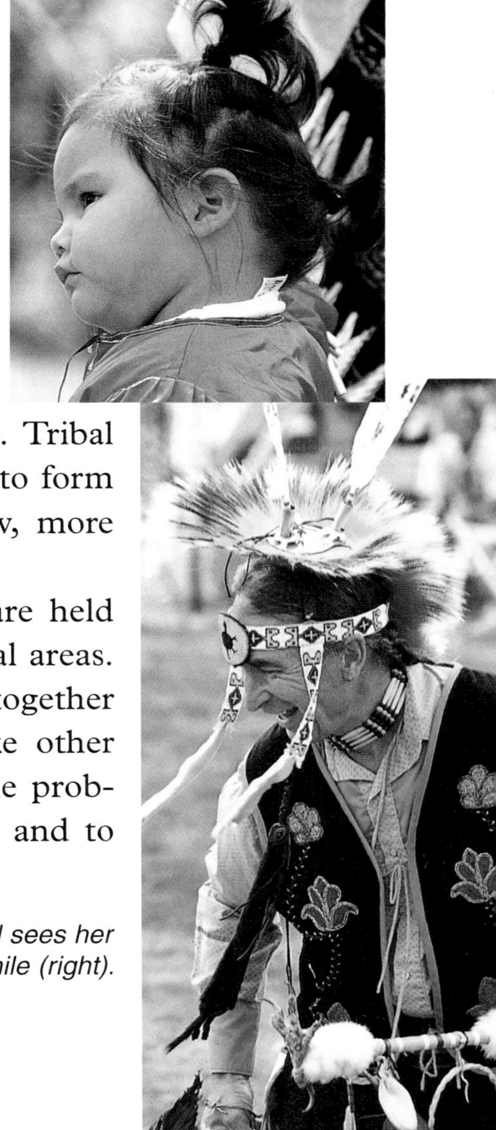

A powwow is a time for everyone to have fun. A little girl sees her traditions (above, right), and a man dances with a smile (right).

Ojibwa Vision Prayer

N'daebaub auzhiwi-anungoong	I can see to the other side of the stars
K'gah kikinowaezhigook anungook	The stars will guide you.
N'daebitum auzhiwi-anungoong	I can hear the other side of the stars
K'gauh noondaugook anungook	The stars will hear me.
Kaugigae n'gah daebitaugoos	Timeless is my voice.
K'gah waussae/aubindum nebau/in	Even in sleep you will perceive,
K'gah gawaek-oshae nebau/in	In sleep you will hear,
Ae-naubindumun dah izhi-waebat	What you dream will be,
K'zhawaenimik Kitche Manitou	The Great Mystery is generous with you.
Maukinauk k'gah mizhinawae/ik	Through the turtle will you speak,
Tchi mino-dodomun, k'bawaudjigae	For good will you dream.
Nindo-waewaemishinaung	Call us.

From: Basil Johnston, *Ojibwa Ceremonies*. Lincoln, NB: University of Nebraska Press, 1990.

Ojibwa Recipe

Maple Sugar Taffy

Adult supervision is required.

1. Heat real maple syrup in a saucepan, until it begins to boil.
2. As it boils, stir constantly until it starts forming threads on the spoon.
3. Before it cools, pour it over a bowl of fresh snow. It will quickly become stringy, sort of like sugary spaghetti.
4. Before the strings harden, take a lollipop stick and roll the strings into a ball around it. Then you have your own lollipop!

Maple sugar taffy is sweet and yummy!

Ojibwa Game

Moccasin Game

The moccasin game was a game of chance. It was most often played by men but could also be played by children. Usually there was a large crowd of observers who would cheer and bet on their favorite team. There were many variations to this game but the rules remained the same.

The game consists of two teams with two players per team and one scorekeeper. Each player acts as either the "hider" or the "guesser" in the game. The hider takes four marbles and hides them in four moccasin-shaped pouches (one ball per moccasin). One of the marbles should be marked in a special way, or it can be a different color from the other three. The guesser from the other team guesses which moccasin holds the marked marble by pointing at his choice with a special "striking stick." While he makes his choice, his partner can sing to the spirits and beat his drum for support. Each team takes its turn hiding and guessing.

The scorekeeper keeps count of correct and incorrect guesses with twenty counting sticks. The team with the greatest number of correct guesses after twenty rounds is declared the winner.

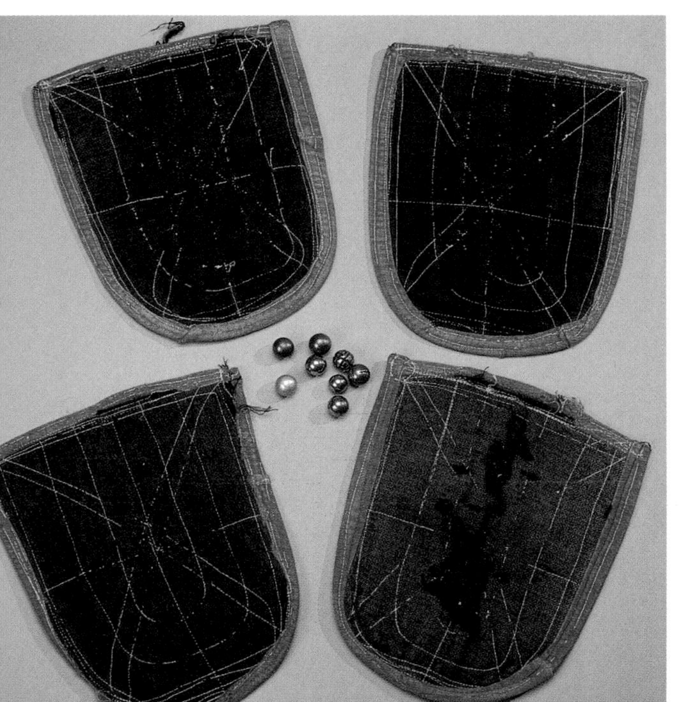

The game pieces from a traditional moccasin game were four moccasin-shaped pouches and musket balls instead of marbles. In this version of the game there are eight balls with one different color ball. This means two balls were placed in each pouch.

Ojibwa Chronology

900	The Ojibwa leave their villages on the Atlantic Coast to travel inland along the St. Lawrence River.
1400	Descendants of those who started out reach their final destination of Madeline Island at the Western corner of Lake Superior, near Ashland, Wisconsin.
1618	The Ojibwa make first contact with French explorers.
1669	Jesuit priest Jacques Marquette establishes a mission near Mackinac called St. Ignace.
1670	Smallpox kills half the Ojibwa living in Sault Sainte Marie.
1687–1690	The Ojibwa push eastward across the northern shores of the Great Lakes to occupy the land of the defeated Iroquois.
1701	The Ojibwa occupy lands from the northern sides of Lake Erie and Ontario to the western shores of Lake Superior. Official trade with the French stops by order of the King of France. The Ojibwa take their furs to the British.
1701–1715	The Ojibwa gradually move the hub of the fur trade from Mackinac to Detroit. They push south and west to occupy the lands of the Lakota Sioux, Sauk, and Fox.
1745–1759	The Ojibwa participate in defending Quebec from British takeover. France is eventually defeated in 1759, and Canada becomes British territory.
1763	British Proclamation of 1763 forbids European settlement west of the Appalachians. This protects the Ojibwa from European invasion, but it is broken by American frontiersmen who cross and settle on Indian land.
1775–1783	The American Revolution. The Ojibwa stay out of the conflict for the most part.

1785	The first treaty signed between the Ojibwa and the United States establishes a boundary between Indian and white lands in Ohio. The result is war along the Ohio River between settlers squatting on Indian land and Indians not recognizing the treaty.
1795	The Greenville Treaty gives most of Ohio to the Americans.
1812	The War of 1812 between the British in Canada and the Americans causes the Ojibwa to fight on both sides.
1815–1850	The Ojibwa wage brutal war on the Lakota Sioux. American settlers push west into the territory of both tribes.
1850–1860	The Robertson Treaties take most of the land along the northern shores of the Great Lakes away from the Ojibwa. In the same way, the Ojibwa lose land in Wisconsin and Minnesota.
1867	A treaty with the Minnesota Ojibwa gives them title to White Earth Reservation.
1887	Dawes Act or General Allotment Act says that all land given to Indians must be held by individuals and not held by the tribe as a whole. This allows land not in the name of an Indian individual to be sold to Americans.
1890–1960s	Ojibwa children are sent away to residential schools. There they are taught to be ashamed of their Indian heritage.
1968	American Indian Movement is formed (AIM). Its goals are to protect Indian people from discrimination by white people and to fight for the return of land and treasures that were stolen from the Native Americans.
1973	A group of Indian activists occupied the Wounded Knee site, where in 1890 about 300 Dakota Sioux had been gunned down by U.S. troops.
1984	Anishinaabe Akeeng, a grassroots movement to get back the land base of White Earth Reservation, is formed.
1994	The Ojibwa of Ipperwash, Ontario, reclaim the land that the Canadian Department of Defence took for use in World War II.

Glossary

American Indian Movement (AIM) An organization founded in the late 1960s to challenge the government of the United States on issues of human rights for all Indian nations, broken treaties, and stealing of sacred land.

Anishinaabe (ah-nish-ih-NAH-bay) Human being, one lowered to Earth by the Creator. This is what the Ojibwa or Chippewa call themselves.

Blackrobes or **Mukadayikonayayg** (muk-ah-DAY-e-CONE-ay-yag) The name the Ojibwa gave to Jesuit priests.

Breechcloth A simple garment worn by men in the summer.

Bubonic plague A contagious disease that causes swollen lymph nodes, fever, weakness, delirium, and finally death.

Cholera A disease passed through contaminated water and food.

Deer sinew The tendon of a deer. It is dried and split lengthwise into thin strips for sewing together animal hide.

Dodaem (doe-DAME) A group of persons within the same family who take a name based on a special animal spirit.

Gitchi Manitou (gih-chee MAN-ih-toe) The Greatest of all the Manitou, the Creator of all things including all the rest of the Manitou. It also translates as "The Great Mystery."

Manitou (MAN-ih-toe) A supernatural spirit. It can also mean mysterious, holy, or mystical.

Manomin (mah-NO-men) Wild rice. This was a staple food of the Ojibwa.

Megis (MAY-gis) A seashell from the cowrie family. The Sacred Megis was said to be a giant seashell that led the Ojibwa to the inland home chosen for them by the Gitchi Manitou.

Mide (MEE-day) A member of the Grand Medicine Society (Midewiwin). This person is a healer, shaman, and priest all rolled into one.

Midewiwin Society (MEE-day-wee-win) The Grand Medicine Society. This organization takes care of the medical and spiritual needs of the people.

Moccasin Footwear made of soft flexible leather without a heel or a sole.

Nanaboozhoo (NAHN-a-boo-zho) An important Manitou who was responsible for creating all life.

Nettle-stalk fiber The stem of the nettle plant. It was split into thick twine.

Ogimah (OH-ghee-mah) A leader appointed by the community to lead them in a special project or to help solve a particular problem.

Prophecy A statement about what will happen in the future.

Reservation Land set aside by the U.S. and Canadian governments for Indians to live on.

Residential schools Schools built by either the government or religious orders for the education and blending of Indian children into white, Christian culture. They were usually boarding schools.

Sacred bundles Relics of ancestors and important things believed to be holy were wrapped in deerskin and handed down within a family from generation to generation. They were used in ceremonies to talk to ancestors who were dead or to mark an important event.

Sacred Circle All life, all things of importance and mystery are viewed as existing in a circle. The circle represents the connection of all things to each other for survival.

Seven Fires The name given to the seven prophecies of the Ojibwa.

Smallpox A very contagious disease, often deadly. Survivors were left with deep scars.

Tuberculosis A highly contagious disease caused by bacteria. Vaccinations are now given to prevent it.

Wigwaum (WEEG-wahm) The most popular house built by the Ojibwa. It was oblong in shape with one door facing east and a rounded top.

Further Reading

Bial, Raymond. *The Ojibwe.* Tarrytown, NY: Benchmark, 2000.

Erdrich, Louise. *The Birchbark House.* New York: Hyperion, 1999.

Gerber, Carole. *Firefly Night.* Dallas: Whispering Coyote, 2000.

Osinski, Alice. *The Chippewa.* Danbury, CT: Children's, 1987.

Osofsky, Audrey. *Dreamcatcher.* New York: Orchard, 1992.

Rendon, Marcie R. *Powwow Summer: A Family Celebrates the Circle of Life.* Minneapolis: Carolrhoda, 1996.

Wittstock, Laura Waterman. *Ininatig's Gift of Sugar: Traditional Native Sugarmaking.* Minneapolis: Lerner, 1993.

Sources

Books:

Benton-Banai, Edward. *The Mishomis Book: The Voice of the Ojibwa.* St. Paul, MN: Red School House, 1988.

Densmore, Frances. *Chippewa Customs.* St. Paul, MN: Minnesota Historical Press, 1979.

Johnston, Basil. *The Manitous: The Spiritual World of the Ojibwa.* New York: HarperCollins, 1995.

Johnston, Basil. *Ojibwa Heritage.* Lincoln, NB: University of Nebraska Press, 1990.

Vizenor, Gerald. *The People Named the Chippewa: Narrative Histories.* Minneapolis, MN: University of Minnesota Press, 1984.

Websites:

Bug-O-Nay-Geeshig: Hole-in-the-Day: Minnesota Ojibwa Chief (extracted from Indian Heroes and Great Chieftains [1916] by Dr. Charles A. Eastman)
http://indy4.fdl.cc.mn.us/~isk/stories/holeday.html

Norval Morrisseau: Biography
http://indy4.fdl.cc.mn.us/~isk/art/morriss/morr_bio.html

The Seven Fires Prophecies of the Anishinabe
www.alphacdc.com/alpha/eldp1.html

Index

Numbers in italics indicate illustration or map.